For my Honey Bunny, Kent
Brendan & H.V.
Mom & Dad
Dom Dom
– D.K.

For Katie & Megan
Mum & Dad
Thank you for all your support.
Lots of love x
– G.C.

POBBOLINA

DIANE KWON
ILLUSTRATED BY GARETH CONWAY

At the Pebbleton school, there was a witch named Pobbolina. Pobbolina disliked children, but this hadn't always been the case.

Years ago, Pobbolina loved children!
When the school was looking for a
new cafeteria lady, she knew it was
the perfect job for her.

Pobbolina spent hours creating recipes and cooking
for the children.

At first, the children loved eating her food which
made her very happy.

But with each passing school year, Pobbolina noticed that the children forgot their manners. There were no more pleases and thank-yous. The children asked for macaroni and cheese instead.

Pobbolina felt unappreciated and unloved. Every time a child forgot their manners, her mouth turned into a deeper frown. Soon she stopped cooking with happiness which made her food taste terrible. When Pobbolina heard a student saying, "Pee-ew! I'd rather eat worms!" she decided enough was enough!

The next morning, Pobbolina walked into the kitchen and took out her book of magic spells.

She flipped through the pages until she found the recipe for Hoppity Floppity Stew.

"Any child who eats this *special* lunch will turn into a bunny! Poor manners no more!"

Pobbolina took out a large pot and gathered the ingredients:

a bunch of carrots,
a pinch of salt, licorice,
butter, pepper, and
a pigeon feather!

She stirred and chanted,
"Cackle, hackle, cackle. Stir, stir, swirl.
Turn these children into bunnies. Let's give this spell a whirl!"

POOF!

Pink smoke filled the kitchen.
Pobbolina's Hoppity Floppity Stew was ready!
She prepared the bowls and trays for lunchtime.

Meanwhile, in the schoolyard, a new student named Franny Anne sat on a bench. She was too shy to introduce herself to her classmates.

Franny Anne watched the other children enjoying recess. She wanted to join in their game of tag, but she did not feel brave enough to ask. Her day already felt like a disaster! Earlier, in art class, her neighbor had asked, "What is your favorite color?" but instead of answering, "Blue," she had blurted out, "Pretzels!" "Will I ever make any friends?" Franny Anne wondered sadly.

PRETZELS!

Franny Anne was especially nervous about lunch. Who would sit next to her? Scared at the thought of sitting alone, Franny Anne hid in the bathroom while the other children lined up for lunch.

Back in the cafeteria, Pobbolina heard the pitter patter of feet. She quickly put on her chef's hat and apron and poured Hoppity Floppity Stew into the lunch bowls.

When the students saw their lunch, they could not help but make a face. The stew was green and smelled sour, but the children were hungry and ate their food quickly. They munched, crunched, and gobbled. Before they could put away their trays, their noses began to itch and twitch.

One girl shouted, "Hey! I'm growing whiskers! Help!" Before she could finish her sentence, she and the rest of her classmates had turned into bunnies and were hopping around the cafeteria.

Pobbolina was thrilled and screamed, "SUCCESS!" Her spell had worked! She took a small pot and a wooden spoon and started drumming.

Franny Anne heard the noises all the way from the bathroom and wondered, "What's going on?" Curious, she walked down the empty hallway towards the loud sounds.

When Franny Anne reached the cafeteria, she was shocked to see that the room was filled with bunnies. She heard Pobbolina scream, "Thanks to my book of magic spells, my feelings will never be hurt again! Bunnies can't forget to say their pleases and thank-yous! Now, if you will excuse me, my furry friends, I am going to rest. I'll see you after my nap."

Franny Anne could not believe it! Pobbolina had turned her classmates into bunnies! She quietly opened the door. One by one, the bunnies hopped over to her, jumping up and down to get her attention. "If I turned into a bunny, I would certainly want someone to help me," Franny Anne thought. She was nervous, but she knew she had to do something. If she did not, how would her classmates see their families again?

She took a deep breath and cleared her throat, "Listen friends!" All the bunnies looked at her. "Let's work together to find a way to turn you back into children! We need Pobbolina's book of magic spells! Who is with me?"

The bunnies raised their paws in the air. "All right then! Come with me!" she said. The bunnies followed Franny Anne into the kitchen. As they looked around, they saw Pobbolina taking a nap in the back room with the book of magic spells on her lap!

"Oh no! What should we do?" Franny Anne thought. She felt a tug on her sock and saw one bunny holding an oven mitt and another pointing at the book of magic spells. "Great idea! Let's make the switch!" Franny Anne whispered.

Franny Anne tiptoed over to Pobbolina. She carefully picked up the book of magic spells from the witch's lap while the bunnies replaced it with the oven mitt. Then they hurried back to the kitchen.

Franny Anne flipped through the pages and whispered, "Look! I found the recipe! Pitter Patter Pancake Batter: flour, butter, a pinch of cinnamon, one egg, milk, and a hair of a hare."

"Let's hop to it!" she said. Franny Anne and the bunnies gathered the ingredients and took turns mixing them in a bowl. They poured the batter into a frying pan and waited for the pancake to turn golden brown. Then with a FLIP, the Pitter Patter Pancake was ready!

Franny Anne placed the plate on the floor, and the bunnies huddled around. They nibbled, munched, and gobbled. Their noses began to itch and twitch. Then POOF! Pink smoke filled the kitchen.

It worked! The children touched their faces and hugged each other. Then they turned to Franny Anne and said, "You are a true friend! Thank you so much for helping us!"

Franny Anne was so happy! Just that morning, she did not have anyone to play with, and now everyone was hugging and thanking her! She started to speak but then – *SNNOOoooOORReee.*

The children were startled! One boy jumped back and knocked over Pobbolina's pot of Hoppity Floppity Stew. It fell to the floor with a loud crash, and the children ran and hid.

Pobbolina's eyes flew open! "What was that noise?!" She walked towards the kitchen and noticed the empty plate on the floor. Then she saw bunny tracks where the children had spilled flour. "What is going on here?!" she yelled as she ran over to examine the mess.

She was in such a rush
that she tripped over
the pot and – SPLASH
– landed face first in a
puddle of the Hoppity
Floppity Stew!

Pobbolina's nose began to itch and twitch, and before she could speak another word – POOF!

There was a giant cloud of pink smoke and sitting on the floor was…a GREEN BUNNY!

The next morning, everyone welcomed Franny Anne with a happy hello and a big hug. At recess, she played tag. In art class, she drew a picture with her neighbor. At lunch, she sat at a table full of friends.

But the most exciting part of the day was taking care of the new class pet – Pobbolina the bunny.

At first, the grumpy green bunny refused to eat. The children did not give up on her and prepared a variety of foods: carrots, asparagus, and apples. They brushed her fur, gave her chew toys, and made her a cozy bed.

All day long, the children took great care of Pobbolina and showered her with love. With each kind gesture, her face softened, and her frown disappeared.

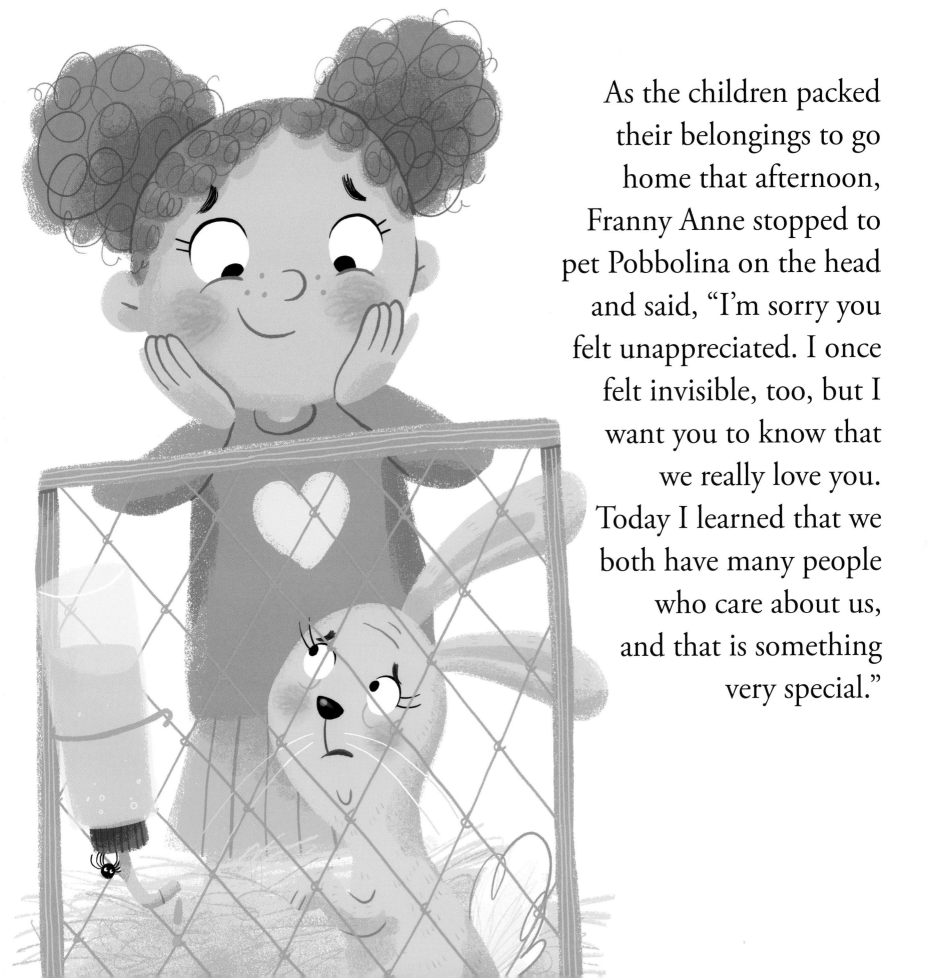

As the children packed their belongings to go home that afternoon, Franny Anne stopped to pet Pobbolina on the head and said, "I'm sorry you felt unappreciated. I once felt invisible, too, but I want you to know that we really love you. Today I learned that we both have many people who care about us, and that is something very special."

As Pobbolina watched Franny Anne leave, she felt her heart grow as big as the moon. Although they sometimes forgot to say please and thank you, the children were very thoughtful, caring, and sweet. Pobbolina wished she had remembered to look beyond their poor manners and deeper into their hearts!

Pobbolina carefully lifted the latch on her cage and quietly hopped to the cafeteria. She searched every nook and cranny until she found her book of magic spells.

The next morning, the children entered the classroom and found the empty cage. "Where is Pobbolina?" they asked.

Suddenly, the children smelled something delicious coming from the hallway.

They saw the cafeteria doors swing open. It was Pobbolina! She was smiling and holding a basket of carrot muffins. The children ran and said, "Thank you, Pobbolina!"

"You are very welcome," Pobbolina said sweetly as she handed them each a breakfast treat.

When she saw Franny Anne, Pobbolina reached out one arm and gave her a big hug. She said, "Thank you for helping me, too."

Then the children headed off to recess, and Pobbolina walked back to the cafeteria. There, she took out her book of magic spells and read over her new recipe – Honey Bunny Carrot Muffins: flour, carrots, cinnamon, sugar, and a pound of happiness, love, and friendship.

As she closed the book and placed it on the shelf, she could have sworn she felt an **itch**, but nothing could distract her from how happy she felt.

Published by Honey Bunny Books, an imprint of Brisance Books Group LLC

Honey Bunny Books is a trademark owned by Diane Kwon.
The publisher is not responsible for websites or their content that are not owned by the publisher.

Honey Bunny Books may be purchased in bulk at special discounts
for sales promotion, corporate gifts, fundraising, or educational purposes.

Brisance Books Group for Honey Bunny Books
21001 N. Tatum Blvd.
Phoenix, AZ 85050

Visit HoneyBunnyBooks.com

Printed in the United States of America
First Edition: October 2020
Hardcover ISBN: 978-1-944194-75-8

Illustrations by Gareth Conway
Cover design and interior production by PCI Publishing Group LLC